Dear Parents:

Congratulations! Your child is taking the first steps on an exciting journey. The destination? Independent reading!

STEP INTO READING® will help your child get there. The program offers five steps to reading success. Each step includes fun stories and colorful art or photographs. In addition to original fiction and books with favorite characters, there are Step into Reading Non-Fiction Readers, Phonics Readers and Boxed Sets, Sticker Readers, and Comic Readers—a complete literacy program with something to interest every child.

Learning to Read, Step by Step!

Ready to Read   Preschool–Kindergarten
• big type and easy words • rhyme and rhythm • picture clues
For children who know the alphabet and are eager to begin reading.

Reading with Help   Preschool–Grade 1
• basic vocabulary • short sentences • simple stories
For children who recognize familiar words and sound out new words with help.

Reading on Your Own   Grades 1–3
• engaging characters • easy-to-follow plots • popular topics
For children who are ready to read on their own.

Reading Paragraphs   Grades 2–3
• challenging vocabulary • short paragraphs • exciting stories
For newly independent readers who read simple sentences with confidence.

Ready for Chapters   Grades 2–4
• chapters • longer paragraphs • full-color art
For children who want to take the plunge into chapter books but still like colorful pictures.

STEP INTO READING® is designed to give every child a successful reading experience. The grade levels are only guides; children will progress through the steps at their own speed, developing confidence in their reading. The F&P Text Level on the back cover serves as another tool to help you choose the right book for your child.

Remember, a lifetime love of reading starts with a single step!

© MGA Entertainment, Inc.
L.O.L. SURPRISE!™ is a trademark of MGA in the U.S. and other countries. All logos, names, characters, likenesses, images, slogans, and packaging appearance are the property of MGA. Used under license by Penguin Random House LLC. Published in the United States by Random House Children's Books, a division of Penguin Random House LLC, 1745 Broadway, New York, NY 10019, and in Canada by Penguin Random House Canada Limited, Toronto.
Step into Reading, Random House, and the Random House colophon are registered trademarks of Penguin Random House LLC.

Visit us on the Web!
StepIntoReading.com
rhcbooks.com

Educators and librarians, for a variety of teaching tools, visit us at RHTeachersLibrarians.com
ISBN 978-0-593-90211-0 (trade) — ISBN 978-0-593-90212-7 (lib. bdg.)
ISBN 978-0-593-90213-4 (ebook)
Printed in the United States of America
10 9 8 7 6 5 4 3 2 1

2025 Random House Children's Books Edition

Random House Children's Books supports the First Amendment and celebrates the right to read.

STEP INTO READING — STEP 3 — READING ON YOUR OWN

WE ARE FAMILY

by B. B. Arthur

Random House 🏠 New York

Did you know the cuties of L.O.L. Surprise! have sisters? They have brothers and pets, too!

Even their besties are like family.
When they are all together,
they are one big happy family!

Life is sweet in Bon Bon's family. They dress alike in pretty pastels. Their candy-colored ways show everyone how sweet sisters and brothers can be!

The family that spins together wins together. D.J. and her family all love music. Even their pets spin records! Every day is a party at their house.

Catch this finned family
by the sea!
Merbaby, Merboi,
and their baby sister
swim and splash all day.

The whole family hangs at the beach. Even Merkitty loves water more than any cat.

Other families like to hang on the court! Hoops MVP and her sisters love to shoot hoops with their brother, Dribbles.

Hoops MVP's friends in the Athletic Club are like family, too! Their amazing teamwork makes them besties for life.

Queen Bee and her hive stick together like honey. They are always fierce, but they never sting.

Sometimes your opposites can become like family. That is what Opposites Club is all about.

Dawn and Dusk, Bashful and Bold—these cuties are just like sisters.

Downtown Doll knows where to find her brothers and sisters. That's in the big city! The busy streets feel like home. It's where these stylish siblings show off their fresh fashion.

Baby Cat and her family all agree on one thing: Cats are the best!

Their favorite styles feature pointy ears and long whiskers. Even their dog thinks cats are *purr*-fect!

Bhaddie loves her wicked siblings. Her brother and sisters tell the best bedtime stories. They are a little spooky and a little wild!

Bhad Gurl has even more sisters. They are sisters who rock!

They write songs together, practice together, and rock together! Playing in a band makes these besties like family.

Can you see
what the Neon family
has in common?
When they are together,
life is brighter than ever!

This family is so bright, their hamster wears shades!

No job is too big for the Can Do family. Can Do Baby and Gear Guy can do anything.

At home or in the S.T.E.M. club, these helpful siblings can take on any project!

These families share hobbies.

They share clubs.

They share talent and style.

They share everything!

The L.O.L. family sticks together—forever!